The Kingdom of Singing Birds

by Miriam Aroner
Illustrated by Shelly O. Haas

Kar•Ben Copies, Inc., Rockville, MD

To my wonderful children, Sarah and Jonathan
—M.A.

To M.K. who lives in the spirit of Zusya
With special thanks to Madeline and Judye
—S.O.H.

Library of Congress Cataloging-in-Publication Data

Aroner, Miriam.
  The kingdom of singing birds/Miriam Aroner and Shelly O. Haas.
      p.   cm.
  Summary: When his collection of rare and exotic birds refuses to sing, the king calls wise Rabbi Zusya for help.
    ISBN 0-929371-43-7: — ISBN 0-929371-46-1 (pbk.):
    [1. Birds—Fiction. 2. Jews—Fiction.] I. I. Haas, Shelly O.   II. Title.
PZ7.A7425K1   1993
[E]—dc20   92-39382
                                                                            CIP
                                                                            AC

Published by KAR-BEN COPIES, INC., Rockville, MD 1-800-4-KARBEN
Printed in the United States of America.

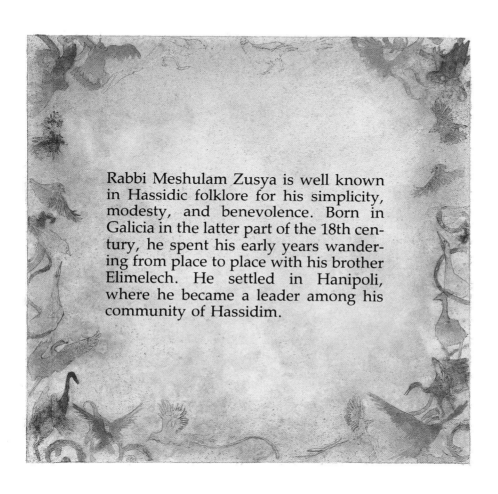

Rabbi Meshulam Zusya is well known in Hassidic folklore for his simplicity, modesty, and benevolence. Born in Galicia in the latter part of the 18th century, he spent his early years wandering from place to place with his brother Elimelech. He settled in Hanipoli, where he became a leader among his community of Hassidim.

Long ago, in a little village in a faraway land, a gentle rabbi named Zusya wondered about the world he lived in.

He noticed stones that no one else thought were special.

He discovered the first spring flowers in their hiding places.

He observed birds nesting way up in the mountains, where the other villagers were too lazy or too busy to climb.

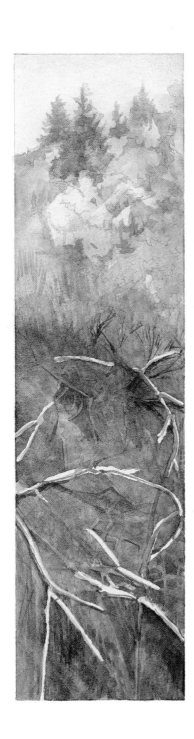

Zusya was always asking questions. Why do things fall down instead of up? Where does the sun go when it sets? What's beyond the moon and stars?

The more Zusya asked, the more he learned. Thus he grew wise in the ways of nature.

Zusya's neighbors would come to him for advice. If their cows refused to give milk, or their orchards failed to bear fruit, Zusya would tell them what they must do.

Now it happened that a new king ruled Zusya's country. His father, the former king, and his grandfather, the old king, had collected birds from all over the world:

> Booby and cuckoo, quetzal and coot. . .
> Cockatoo, bobolink, parakeet, goose. . .
> Dickeybird, chickadee, curlew and crane. . .
> Widgeon and pigeon, bluebird and jay. . .

The birds were very beautiful, but they did not sing.

This troubled the young king, for he loved birds as much for their music as for their beauty. He asked his advisors how to make them sing.

"Give them treats," said one.

So the king fed his birds the juiciest berries, the crunchiest seeds, and the sweetest mountain water in the land. The birds ate and drank. But they did not sing.

"Build them a bigger, fancier house," suggested another.

So the king ordered his craftsmen to build an aviary ten times taller and twenty times wider, and to decorate it with gold and silver and jewels. The birds flew higher and farther in their new home, but still they did not sing.

"Find them mates," said a third advisor.

So the king sent his bird catchers everywhere, even up into the mountains. But the new birds were as silent as the old.

"I will give a barrel of gold to anyone who can make my birds sing," proclaimed the young ruler.

From all over the kingdom, people came to try.

Magicians did tricks for the birds. Acrobats tumbled and clowns stumbled. Jugglers juggled and fiddlers fiddled. A witch even cast a spell!

But the birds remained silent.

"My birds will never sing," sighed the king. "As it was in my father's time and in my grandfather's time, so it shall be in mine."

One day, one of the palace musicians said, "I have heard that in a village near my own lives a gentle rabbi named Zusya, wise in the ways of nature. He once got a farmer's hen to lay her eggs, after everyone else had given up. Perhaps he could get your birds to sing."

So the king sent his servants to find Zusya and bring him to the palace.

Zusya was excited and a little scared. He had never been very far from home. What could he, a simple man from a tiny village, tell a king? Then he remembered, "Although I haven't traveled far *from* my village, I've traveled a lot *inside* it. I know what I know. Even a king can't know everything. Besides, if a king summons, a wise man goes."

So Zusya journeyed many days and nights. He followed the king's men across rivers, through forests, and high up into the mountains.

Finally they reached the palace. It was even more magnifi-
cent than Zusya had imagined. And the royal aviary! Zusya
had never seen so many kinds of birds!

Treebirds and seabirds, red, green, and blue. . .
Shorebirds and snowbirds, so lovely to view. . .

From India, Arabia, the wide world around. . .
A rainbow of colors—but alas, not a sound!

Such glorious birds, but not a chirp or a peep! Zusya
thought about the birds that sang in his village, and up in
the mountains, and all along his journey.

There was something he must tell the king, even if it made him angry.

"Come closer, Zusya," beckoned the king. "I have been told that you are wise. Can you make my birds sing?"

"Your Majesty," began Zusya. "You won't like what I have to say."

"Say it anyway," demanded the king.

"Your Majesty, if you want your birds to sing, you must let them go free."

"What? Free my birds? Impossible!" roared the king. "My birds are my treasure. My father, and his father, and his father's father always kept birds."

"And did their birds sing?" asked Zusya.

"No, but. . ."

"You are king now," said Zusya. "You must do things your way."

"But my way is their way," insisted the young ruler.

"Then your birds will be like theirs. Silent."

The king yearned to hear his birds sing. But he was afraid of losing them.

"What if they all fly away?" he thought.

He walked around and around the aviary, looking at his lovely, silent birds. What should he do?

He opened the aviary a bit. One tiny bird flew out and perched in a tree. For the very first time the king heard it sing.

"Listen, Zusya," he exclaimed. "Listen to that bird!"

The king opened the door a little wider. A few more birds flew out and they, too, began to sing.

He gathered a few feathers that had fallen to the ground. ''To remember my beautiful birds,'' he said sadly to Zusya.

Then the king opened the aviary all the way.

When all the birds were free, the palace was filled with singing, lovelier than any music he, or his father, or his father's father had ever heard.

The king looked up at the sky, in all directions, as far as he could see. "My birds," he cried. "My precious birds!"

Eagle and egret, linnet and loon. . .
Sparrow, canary, cardinal, tern. . .
Oriole, whippoorwill, nightingale, gull. . .
Raven and falcon, plover and dove. . .

Some birds flew away.

But some birds stayed. And when birds in other countries heard about the king who let his birds go free, they came to settle in his kingdom. In time, there were so many birds and so much singing that the country became known as the Kingdom of Singing Birds.

And Zusya? He used his reward wisely, to help the poor people in his village. He was invited often to the palace as the king's special advisor. And whenever Zusya visited he traveled a different road, so he could see new places and learn new things along the way.

ABOUT THE AUTHOR

Miriam Aroner was born in Chicago and has lived and worked in Boston, New York, and Israel. Her articles and poetry have been published in a number of journals. The mother of twins, she lives in El Cerrito, CA.

ABOUT THE ILLUSTRATOR

Shelly O. Haas was raised in a home where the arts were very important. She earned a BFA in Illustration from the Rhode Island School of Design. She has illustrated five books for Kar-Ben including *Daddy's Chair*, which won the 1992 Sydney Taylor Award from the Association of Jewish Libraries. She lives in Michigan with her son.